Ours?

THIS BOOK BELONGS
TO

children's choice®

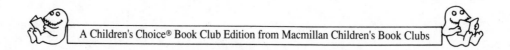

The Dinosaur Who Lived In My Backyard

B.G. HENNESSY · Pictures by SUSAN DAVIS

VIKING KESTREL

VIKING KESTREL

Viking Penguin Inc., 40 West 23rd Street, New York, New York 10010, U.S.A.

Penguin Books Ltd, 27 Wrights Lane, London W8 5TZ (Publishing & Editorial), and Harmondsworth, Middlesex, England (Distribution & Warehouse)

Penguin Books Australia Ltd, Ringwood, Victoria, Australia

Penguin Books Canada Limited, 2801 John Street, Markham, Ontario, Canada L3R 1B4

Penguin Books (N.Z.) Ltd, 182–190 Wairau Road, Auckland 10, New Zealand

Text copyright © B.G. Hennessy, 1988
Illustrations copyright © Susan Davis, 1988
All rights reserved
First published in 1988 by Viking Penguin Inc.
Published simultaneously in Canada

Set in Garamond #3
10 9 8 7 6 5 4 3

Library of Congress Cataloging in Publication Data
Hennessy, Barbara.   The dinosaur who lived in my backyard / by Barbara Hennessy; illustrated by Susan Davis.
p.   cm.
Summary: A young boy imagines what it was like long ago when a dinosaur lived in his backyard.
ISBN 0-670-81685-X
[1. Dinosaurs—Fiction.] I. Davis, Susan, 1948–   ill.   II. Title.
PZ7.H3914Di 1988   [E]—dc19   87-19867

For Matthew
and every other child
who has wished for a dinosaur of their own.
B.G.H.

For Jake
who taught me about dinosaurs
when he was four year old,
and for Jessica, John and Fes.
With love.
S.D.

There used to be a dinosaur who lived in my backyard.
Sometimes I wish he still lived here.

The dinosaur who lived here
hatched from an egg that was
as big as a basketball.

By the time he was five, he was as big as our car.

Just one of his dinosaur feet
was so big it wouldn't even have
fit in my sandbox.

My mother says that if you eat all your vegetables you'll grow
very strong. That must be true, because that's all this dinosaur ate.
I bet he ate a hundred pounds of vegetables every day.
That's a whole lot of lima beans.

This dinosaur was so heavy that he would have made my whole neighborhood shake like pudding if he jumped. He weighed as much as twenty pick-up trucks.

The dinosaur who lived in my backyard
was bigger than my school-bus.
Even bigger than my house.

He had many other dinosaur friends.

Sometimes they played
hide-and-seek.

Sometimes they had terrible fights.

The dinosaur who used to live here was allowed to sleep outside every night. It's a good thing he didn't need a tent. He was so big he would have needed a circus tent to keep him covered.

Back when my dinosaur lived here,
my town was a big swamp.
This dinosaur needed a lot of water.
If he still lived here we'd have to keep
the sprinkler on all the time.

My dinosaur had a very long neck so he could eat the leaves at the top of trees. If he still lived here, I bet he could rescue my kite.

That's all I know about the dinosaur who used to live in my backyard.

He hasn't been around
for a very long time.
Sometimes I wish he
still lived here.

It would be pretty hard to keep a dinosaur happy.
But my sister and I are saving all our lima beans—
just in case.